For Nicole and Jason

First published in the United States of America in June 2016
by Bloomsbury Children's Books
www.bloomsbury.com

Bloomsbury is a registered trademark of Bloomsbury Publishing Plc

For information about permission to reproduce selections from this book, write to Permissions, Bloomsbury Children's Books, 1385 Broadway, New York, New York 10018

Bloomsbury books may be purchased for business or promotional use. For information on bulk purchases please contact Macmillan Corporate and Premium Sales Department at specialmarkets@macmillan.com

Library of Congress Cataloging-in-Publication Data
Names: Yoon, Salina, author, illustrator.
Title: Bear's big day / by Salina Yoon.
Description: New York : Bloomsbury, [2016].
Summary: Bear, feeling very grown-up, says good-bye to his stuffed rabbit, Floppy, and starts his first day of school but soon he is missing Floppy and worrying that he is not ready to be a big bear, after all.
Identifiers: LCCN 2015036451
ISBN 978-0-8027-3832-5 (hardcover) • ISBN 978-0-8027-3834-9 (e-book) • ISBN 978-0-8027-3835-6 (e-PDF)
Subjects: | CYAC: First day of school—Fiction. | Schools—Fiction. | Bears—Fiction. | Toys—Fiction. | JUVENILE FICTION/Animals/Bears. | JUVENILE FICTION/Social Issues/Friendship. | JUVENILE FICTION/School & Education.
Classification: LCC PZ7.Y817 Bef 2016 | DDC [E]—dc23
LC record available at http://lccn.loc.gov/2015036451

Art created digitally using Adobe Photoshop
Typeset in Triplex Sans
Book design by Salina Yoon and Colleen Andrews
Printed in China by Leo Paper Products, Heshan, Guangdong
1 3 5 7 9 10 8 6 4 2

All papers used by Bloomsbury Publishing, Inc., are natural, recyclable products made from wood grown in well-managed forests. The manufacturing processes conform to the environmental regulations of the country of origin.

BEAR'S BIG DAY

Salina Yoon

BLOOMSBURY

NEW YORK   LONDON   OXFORD   NEW DELHI   SYDNEY

It was Bear's big day.

"I can cut my pancakes all by myself,"
said Bear. "I'm a big bear now."

"Yes, you are!" said Mama.

Mama gave him a big-bear backpack.

It had pockets for each of his things.

pencil case

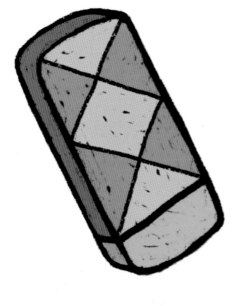

lunch box

crayons

glue

Bear hugged Floppy good-bye.

"You need to stay home," said Bear. "That's what little bunnies do. Big bears go to school."

"I love you, Floppy!"

At school, Bear met his new teacher.

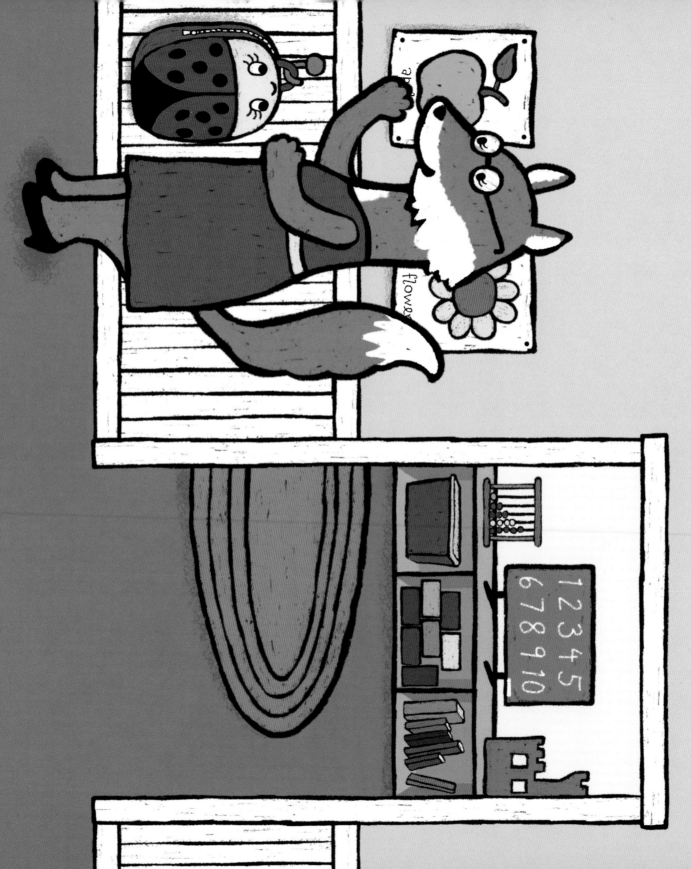

"Welcome to my class," said Miss Fox.

Bear thought school would be lots of fun.
But something—or someone—was missing.

During arts and crafts time, everyone colored but Bear.

At snack time, everyone ate but Bear.

At nap time, everyone slept but Bear.

"What is the matter, Bear?" asked Miss Fox.

"You haven't colored, eaten, or napped!"

"I miss Floppy," said Bear.
"I thought I was ready for school.
I guess I'm not a big bear after all."

"You ARE a big bear! Being big doesn't mean you have to do everything by yourself," said Miss Fox.

"Even big teachers need help sometimes."

Bear thought about Floppy home alone.
Then he had an idea.

He asked Miss Fox for help.

Miss Fox pulled out some supplies, and together they cut, glued, and colored.

After school, Bear was happy to see Floppy.

"Floppy, I made something special for you.
Now, I'm really ready for school!"

Bear had a wonderful time doing big bear things.

apple

Floppy

carrot

So did Floppy.